**Peppa Pig™**

# The Naughty Tortoise

It's autumn and Tiddles the tortoise is going to
sleep for the winter. But Tiddles isn't sleepy,
so he has run away and climbed a tree!
"How are we going to rescue him?" asks Peppa.
"I'll ring the fire brigade," replies Dr Hamster.

"Stand clear!" shouts Mummy Elephant
when the fire engine arrives.
She puts the ladder against the tree, and
Mummy Cow starts to climb up towards Tiddles.

Nee naa!

Nee naa!

Mummy Cow reaches
the top of the ladder, but
Tiddles climbs higher!
"Come here, you little
pickle!" calls Mummy Cow.
"Be careful, Mummy Cow!"
shouts Mummy Elephant.
But Mummy Cow climbs on
to a branch and gets stuck.
Cows are not very good
at climbing trees.

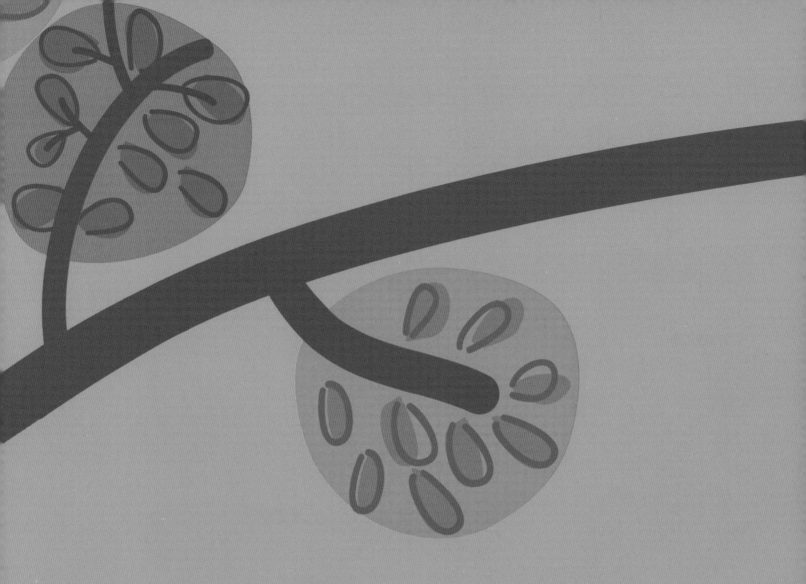

"Hang on!" cries Mummy Elephant. "I'm coming up!"
Mummy Elephant climbs on to a different
branch, and she gets stuck, too!
Elephants are not very good at climbing trees, either.

"What are we going to do now?" asks Peppa.
"I'll call another rescue service," says Dr Hamster.
"Grandad Dog's breakdown truck!"

"Hmm," says Grandad Dog when he arrives.
"How do you get tortoises out of trees?
Shall I climb up?"
"Yes, please," replies Dr Hamster.
Grandad Dog climbs up on to the first
branch in the tree.

"Oh," says Grandad Dog. "I seem to be stuck!"
Dogs are not very good at climbing trees, either.
"Now what are we going to do?" asks Peppa.
"We'll have to call the highest rescue service
in the land!" replies Dr Hamster.

Miss Rabbit arrives in her rescue helicopter.
"Hello, everyone!" she calls down.
"Now, let's rescue this tortoise!"
Miss Rabbit puts her helicopter
on autopilot and climbs down
the ladder to the tree.

"Got you, you little rascal," says Miss Rabbit, reaching out and grabbing Tiddles from the top of the tree. Then she carries him safely down to the ground.

"Thank you for saving my Tiddles, Miss Rabbit,"
says Dr Hamster.
"No problem!" replies Miss Rabbit. Then she
climbs back up the ladder to rescue Mummy
Elephant, Mummy Cow and Grandad Dog.
"Thank you for saving us, too!" they cry.
"Just doing my job!" replies Miss Rabbit.

"What a naughty tortoise
you are!" says Dr Hamster.
Tiddles yawns.
"Oh good, now you're
sleepy," says Dr Hamster.
"Back in your box you go."

"Sleep well, Tiddles!" cries Peppa.
Tiddles has gone to sleep for the winter
and will wake again in the springtime.
"Shhh!" whispers Peppa. Everyone
giggles, very quietly!